Love
ON
Ventilator

Love ON VENTILATOR

DEVI RAGHUVANSHI

PARTRIDGE

To order additional copies of this book, contact
Partridge India
000 800 10062 62
orders.india@partridgepublishing.com

www.partridgepublishing.com/india

DEDICATION

Dedicated to my Parents, who made me to read and write,
while they were just the farmers.

Acknowledgements

I acknowledge and express my gratitude to my wife SUSHMA, for the input, spell check and all the inspiration and ideas, I conceived watching the degree of her patience.

My elder daughter PREETI deserves special mention for the emotional and financial support in bringing out the publication of this book.

I would like PAYAL, my younger daughter to be a partner in my this endeavour. Frankly speaking I have copied some of her blogs to make my book rich and true.

I would also express my special thanks to Mr.Rajesh Chaurasia, my colleague, for typing the entire manuscript.

Finally I thank all my friend on Facebook, my college mates, for encouraging me to write this book. My heartfelt thanks will not be complete unless I mentioned the big help I got from "Bhagvad Gita' and 'Google', the boss for anything.

You all are part of my these efforts BIG or SMALL.

The contents of this story is purely based on the imaginations of the author and it is no way connected with any individual, place or incidence. However any resemblance is coincidental.

The author does not take any responsibility for any damage or loss except he expresses regrets if any.

INTRODUCTION

We hear that love happens only once in your life time. How far this is correct, nobody knows but we still believe so as everyone says in our epics films.

My point of view in this book is not the same as in case of Ajit, the character in my this book, this has happened genuinely for the second time.

You would now say that this isn't love, it is either infatuation or extra marital affair. Extra marital affair for Ajit can neither be accepted nor justified as his intensity of loving Sudha is unmatched. It is divine, unconditional, selfless and with no hope of return.

He says "I am afraid of being rejected yes, I am also afraid of being accepted for wrong reasons."

He also says "please if one of us cries let both of us cry but preferably neither of us."

He also concludes and says "I don't care how hard being together is but nothing worse than being apart is".

CHAPTER 1

STORY BEGINS.............

After completing a successful and satisfying career of 25 years in INDIAN ARMY and obtaining so many gallantry awards , Ajit hung his boots to explore green grass on the other side. He was 55years then.He was popularly known as Col. Ajit Singh.

After retirement from a very hectic life in desert , snow clad mountains, he set out to a mountain with his wife for a pleasure trip.He headed for Kullu , Manali in Himachal Pradesh. The place was nice. The lake in the mountains which according to mythology is one of the emerald eyes of Shiva's wife. A hike or horse back ride to the top of peak, the highest point, provides stunning view of the snowcapped, Himalayas.

After spending two weeks, with lot of ideas for his future plans Ajit came back to DELHI without even slightest idea as what is stored for him in times to come. Most of the time Ajit was on a wild google search as what could be his time schedule so as he does not find his retirement a serious threat of boredom and a catalyst for decay. He remembers that he used to tell everybody that he would like to die on a work-station rather than in home or hospitals. He devised too many options like (1) Get a new assignment (2) Volunteer for some NGOs (3) Pursue some sports like Golf or Tennis (4) Develop a hobby like writing or singing (5) Start a new business (6) Travel and explore India & Foreign land (7) make new friends (8) Be part of your family and grand children

Easiest Ajit felt was to try some NGOs, where he could sincerely contribute something. He went to some hospital and met administrative officer who directed him to a ward to look after terminally ill patients suffering from serious and chronical ailments like cancer etc., and the doctors were sure of their death now or a little later.

Ajit though tried his best to serve such patients but he could not mentally prepare himself to look after them due to pathetic conditions of them. He was not able to justify his roll and purpose, he had gone there so he declined and started exploring other NGO options. He found old age home under helpage India prospectus. He met too many old people from 60 to 95 years and came to know the plight of some of them who were just kept there by their children to shed the basis responsibility of being their sons and daughters and there were few who did not want anything from you except you only give them your time as they do not have people to talk to them. You only have to visit them talk to them on any topic and be part of their conversations. There were some old ladies wanting some medical assistance and companionship. At times you feel that somebody can leave their mother on somebody's mercy. Shame on the sons and daughters who have done this. Ajit was happy to confirm that number of parents was less for daughters as compared to sons. Ajit sometimes used to listen to the comments from his wife that you go to old age home to help those elderly ladies but do you know that you are also one of them, hope some old female just keeps you there as her soulmate and you do not return. Ajit jokingly would tell her that if this happens, I will get her also home and you both can stay as two sisters or may be like Hema & Prakash assuming him to be Dharmendra. Anyway he was regular twice a week and did his best possible and all the people over there were happy with whatever little contribution he could make.

Ajit was slowly coming to terms with his this routine like his sports activities with his grandchildren, newspapers, books & computer etc. While one day he was surfing his mails, he noticed that there was a linked-in message from one Sudha asking him to accept her invitation to confirm his friendship. For a moment he did not understand who Sudha is and why should he confirm his friendship. Normally Ajit is a loner and doesn't become friends unless he is sure of. But the name was sounding a bit familiar so he reached to the profile of the sender.

He did not know whether it was a pleasant surprise or a shock of his life when he read the profile of Sudha. Pleasant in the sense that he knew Sudha for many years as he saw her as an young bride with her husband who was an engineer Trainee in Military Engineering Services, popularly known as M.E.S.and then rose to become Major who had worked under him for few years and shocked to know that she, who was once an young bride is a widow now. He could not bear the turbulence in him and could not know how to react with the circumstances. He was aware of the tragic death of her husband Major Vinod Pradhan who after a service of 10 years with INDIAN ARMY, MES, became a big contractor with MES , CPWD and other Public sector Undertakings who was killed during insurgency in Kabul while he was constructing Govt. buildings and infrastructure facilities in Kabul, Afghanistan and in fact Ajit has visited them along with his wife to Sudha's place for condolences. But a sudden e-mail from Sudha made Ajit NUMB and finally Ajit sent her the mail confirming their linked-in relationship also shared his cell number as requested.

The next day he got a call from Sudha asking him to help in running her contracting company as she was finding it difficult to manage, being absolutely new in this industry and also being a lady. Please note that contracting business is full of cruelty, corruption and cheating and lot of compromises in terms of morality etc. Ajit needed something like this to keep himself busy, earn a bit of money and most importantly help the female in distress who happened to be wife of one of his favourite army officer. He accepted her invitation to meet her in restaurant to discuss the future mode of operations and understand the company status, manpower, liabilities and assets. On a designated day they met in a restaurant for lunch. Sudha was accompanied by one of her family and trusted friend.

Before we move further let me briefly introduce the family status of these two individuals. Ajit, 55 years had two children one elder daughter and younger one a son both professionally qualified, married and working in Silicon Valley U.S.. The son of elder daughter was born with some serious medical deformity and needed 24 hours care. Since all of them were working so they needed Ajit's wife to be with them on 24 hour basis. Ajit could not make it to U.S., as he had lot of liabilities in India so his wife left for U.S. and he was not able to visit U.S. due to property disputes at home and his army obligations.

Whereas Sudha, 38 years widow few months back with two kids daughter and son both 12 & 8 years of age. Everything was good in her family, good reasonably well settled family with house, school going kids etc. but now shattered due to untimely & unexpected death of her husband due to terrorist attack.

On his arrival in this restaurant, he was greeted with smiles by both Sudha & the gentleman accompanying her.

Sudha was looking beautiful, dignified and composed but was not even close to images, Ajit had in his mind when Ajit saw her as an young bride. She was having a very light make up and he could immediately understand that traditionally, when the husband dies the widow he leaves behind is expected to forsake all pleasures including wearing jewellery which often has sacred and status values.

Ajit was explained the details about company and the circumstances which the company was passing through. Everyone working in the company was trying to take his flesh out reasonable and unreasonable knowing that Sudha is ignorant of the company affairs. Some senior people went upto that extent that they started asking for shares or else they would quit and It was becoming very difficult for Sudha to even manage day to day operations. Blackmailing is another word for their this behaviour.

Ajit could see the depth of sorrow in Sudha's eyes however she tried her best to camouflage the reality within. She internally seemed so devasted that she did not made an eye contact even once and the confidence level was zero. Sometimes just because a person looks happy, you will have to look past their smile to see how much pain they may be in. Ajit is a sharp man, emotionally very weak and he felt that he should if he could and bring the company reasonably to a comfort zone. The only professional question Sudha asked, "Col. Sir I do not need your help without a commercial compensation so please let me know how much will it cost me and my company now? He retorted immediately," whatever you are paying to your senior most person General Manager, Director or anybody except you. Anyway the figure was agreed. Though the compensation was too little to discuss, Ajit agreed and made himself understand that you are a retired soul, you will be doing it as part of charity to help this female in distress and you will also be paying homage to the deceased soul, her husband and confirmed his joining the company and put his best efforts. Before leaving the restaurant and finding some moments to talk to her in private Ajit made her at ease by saying that everyone will go through some hard times at some point. Life isn't easy just something to think about. Do you know the people that are strongest are usually the most sensitive. Do you know that the people who exhibit the most kindness are first to get mistreated. Do you know the three hardest things to say are I love you, am sorry and help me. Trust yourself, you will succeed. Ajit was a happy and satisfied man that day. He sensed and saw the first real smile on her face.

Chapter 2

AFTER ONE WEEK........

Ajit joined Sudha's company after a week. He prepared himself to face the major problem on contracts, indisciplined staff abd financial irregularities. More than any thing, Ajit's main responsibility was to put Sudha in a right frame of mind who after a tragic death of her husband few months back, was left to pick up the pieces and move on with her life but she hasn't. She's shut herself to the world and vowed never to love life again.

Another challenge, he was to face was the sagging moral of some of the dedicated workers and the reputation of the company for non-performance. Rising financial burden in form of taxation, vendor payment. The clients were not supportive as the work undertaken by company was either sub-standard or not completed as per mutually agreed terms and conditions of the contracts. This forced the clients not to make even legitimate payments. The consultants & other agencies were also not favouring Ajit.

Different situations are common by product of internal & external changes for examples, Ajit faced difficult situations to arise just before or after something new starts or ends.

During an economic slump that forces new jobs to come, cost cutting measures or when the business is in a period of transition. Many difficult situations center on employee issues such as grievances, inter-personal issues and both warranted unrealistic requests and others included dealing with unhappy customers and also balancing the needs of the department against the needs of business.

Ajit's roll increased to step in when the employees could not resolve issues or calm an extremely unhappy or angry customers. He tried his best using his superior conflict resolution skills. He also tried his best to display a positive attitude, genuine concern and acknowledge the customer feelings.

CHAPTER 3

AFTER A MONTH.............

Reviving this company from the ground up was at times lonely stressful and all consuming. Remembering that you are going to die, is the best way, he knew to avoid trap of thinking, you have something to lose. You are already naked so there is no reason not to follow your heart. Ajit wanted to run this business and be in control of his destiny. He had no idea where it would lead them (Sudha and Ajit) but whatever it was he knew, it has to be better than feeling bored and unfulfilled. He was ready for adventure.

On the day of getting his first big contract he sensed something revolutionary was happening. They both were genuinely excited about their this achievement and they both univocally said that any crusade requires optimism and ambition to aim high. Ajit for the first time saw the genuine smile on her face.

Success has such a wonderful taste that you want to try all of the flavours. For Ajit it was his first taste of success doing something that he loved to do. It gave him a bit of hope and validation that he could do it. This positive energy improved his creativity, boosted his confidence and gave him the drive to taste more success. He pledged to himself that the challenges is in the beginning. Deep down he knew that he is capable of doing great things. Sudha was once told by one of the vendors that you now have Amitabh Bachchan of your industry and shape of things for company will change in the times to come which put an additional burden, responsibility and prestige issue on Ajit.

Ajit started reorganizing systems, culture of the company and held his first open discussion with the entire team to understand them and also share their views with a common intent of bringing this company out of red. His first advice to all was to follow punctuality and discipline. Secondly he defined duties and responsibilities of each and every individual and created departments like Sales & Marketing, Designing & Planning, Project Execution, Procurement & Purchase, H.R. and Accounts. He also defined service department as a separate business centre reporting directly to him. It is not like that these departments were not existing earlier they were but not specifically defined so as to fix responsibility on somebody.

In addition to above, everybody was made responsible for Sales as the need of Sales was of utmost importance. A fresh list of prospective clients, consultants was made on Pan India basis and follow up with these people was planned.

Before we unfold the consequences of follow up of this plan, let me briefly give you the background of Ajit, so that my readers can also understand, justify or criticize the performance of the man who is driving the company.

Ajit before joining this company was on a very senior position in Military Engineering Services(MES) an important arm of INDIAN ARMED FORCES and he was the one who used to appoint Consultants, Project Management Companies (PMCs) and right from small to the biggest companies in this field used to beg for their appointments with him. In short all the Consultants and others used to meet him on weekly basis for their business relations. In the process there were many such people who were not favoured by Ajit not because he had anything adverse against them but simply because even if he wanted to oblige everyone he could not have done. He was honest in this confession.

To pursue the motive of revival of the company Ajit planned his first business meet with one of the Consultants and was accompanied by Sudha. The first meeting with a Client was not like a first date. It was a chance to put your best foot forward and lay the foundation for a successful long term working relationship. Even when the Consultant was very well acquainted with Ajit but the first client meeting was like a job interview. Ajit was well prepared to convey his professionalism inspire confidence and thoroughly convince the Consultants that his job and money is in safe hands. Ajit before meeting this Consultant did a research on them for their past experience with the company and their expectations now.

CHAPTER 4

There was no reason for not awarding us few projects except the answer given by head of the consultancy firm was that Ajit when we approached you in your previous company for awarding consultancy job to us which you could have done, you never gave us an opportunity. Ajit plainly told them that It was just a matter of chance and it was never intentionally denied to you.

In fact it was a sweet revenge for the act when Ajit never did knowingly. Ajit with a little despair left their office and for the first time his ego, was hurt for the wrong reason. Amazingly Sudha felt worse than him and simply told Ajit, I am sorry for this incidence as it was not expected from them. I only told her that this is the beginning. we might have to face much more than this in the times to come.

Ajit for the first time felt that there is more to a professional relationship in both of us.

Ajit explained to Sudha, "If you feel lost, disappointed or weak, return to yourself to you, who you are here and now. When you get there, you will, discover yourself like a lotus flower in full bloom even in a muddy pond, beautiful and strong. Remember there is light always after dark. Next visit after this disappointing first meeting was the site visit of one of his projects which they have recently acquired. The project site was a five star super deluxe hotel in Chandigarh of Indian Tourism Development Corporation, ITDC and an extensive visit was undertaken by Sudha, Ajit and the local execution team. Sudha asked too many questions technical and commercial and she was explained in details. She was also taken to two basements to show how the car park ventilation work was to be carried out by us. The basement was not brightly lit and there was lot of civil construction material lying here & there and it was not easy to move around for Sudha due to high heeled footwear. Ajit offered her his hands as support and Sudha did not feel anything out of place with this skin contact. After the site visit it was the next planning meeting with Project Manager and MD ITDC and we both had to wait in a separate room to get our turn after some more contractors who were already there in the ongoing meeting.

Sudha was calm and composed staring on a board in front of her which contained detailed programme of construction of that project. Ajit knew that she is not understanding on IOTA of MS Project except the start and end date but she was lost in that. Ajit glanced at the profile of Sudha and thought to himself that Sudha was a very attractive and beautiful woman. She was looking stunningly beautiful inspite of having lot of pain and anxiety in her.

Ajit withdrew his thoughts and thought that what is storming his brains, is not right. She needed his moral support not the love which he was thinking. Both of them finished their meeting and proceeded to DELHI.

For Ajit, Sometimes reaching out and taking some one's hand is beginning of a journey. He felt that millions of tiny universes are being born and dying in space between your fingers and her skin and he thought that he could touch anything in the world right now, it would be her heart. Ajit after all is a human being. With these thoughts of pleasure and guilt, they both sat in the car for 5 hours journey together just the twosomes.

To continue the conversation to pass those five hours journey, Ajit asked Sudha about the atmosphere, attitude of her family after the tragedy.

Ajit says, she had a bit of confidence on him to share some of her experiences before and after the tragic death of her husband. She started narrating her past experiences. Her husband was a self-made man, used to love her to the core of his heart. His kids were life to him. The only problem he had, was that he was his mumma's boy. When his mother is around, he will become Shravan Kumar and would not listen to anything or anybody uttering a single word against her even when he was told the truth. She continued, my mom-in-law also became widow at an early age so may be the time had made her. She would always behave and command as if she is only right.

We were maintaining that typical mother-in-law and daughter-in-law relationship. My husband used to fight and sometimes used to become violent even on petty issues involving his mother. I will tell you a specific incidence which is fresh in my mind even now. I was asked to cook meals on 3rd day of the delivery of my first child. I was broken that day.

And after his death, I am yet to experience how the things take shape. So far she has been supportive.

Ajit also shared that he is a simple village boy, became an engineer. Probably nobody in his family even knew the spelling of an engineer. He explained his problems of finances, English language etc. and also how he also became self-made man.

On the way they dropped in a restaurant for dinner. Five minutes later, we ate in a restaurant on highway. We got world's fastest waitor who had us in and out in 45 minutes. It was disappointing but we atleast communicated and the flame was lighted. Sudha was very shy and reserved but Ajit could atleast judge that she is a true coconut, hard from out and soft from within.

They both reached to their place of origin DELHI and next day, they were on job as usual.

Ajit by virtue of his nature was struggling to sustain the operations of the company and was very carefully watching the day to day happening in the industry. He concluded that it is the rule of contracts made up of three words, there is good, cheap and fast. You can have any two, good and cheap won't be fast, good and fast won't be cheap, cheap and fast, won't be good. Ajit always followed the second option, Good and fast and lost many jobs.

People in the market around wanted to get some contracts at any cost and offered cheap and fast option and they were the winners. Unfortunately the supervisors of the projects, consultants & PMCs did lot of compromises with their quality and quantity including measurements. Somehow Ajit never followed and tried these non-ethical contractual ways & means.

The biggest problem Ajit faced was his own ego which was clashing with egos of Clients and Consultants. He was insulted, humiliated for the revenge many people took as they were not given jobs by him in his earlier position. He had to suppress his ego and self-respect many times for no fault of his for Sudha's company to grow but how long? He was also a human being and self-respecting emotional fool and not a machine for on and off.

Another very big challenge for Ajit and the Construction/ Infrastructure projects was lack of skilled work force. This was the biggest challenge for the country also. He know the fact that the biggest challenge is not capital or delayed approvals but skilled manpower. Unskilled workforce, not only delays completion schedule of projects but also results is more material consumption, rework and bad name. The skill scale was not limited to only labour class but equally existing in higher scales including consultants and designers.

Inspite of all these hurdles Ajit and Sudha, were able to book few more jobs but were nowhere close to the target, Ajit set for the company in that financial year. Then they started exploring different segments, different cities and different clients. They both moved to Hyderabad for business promotions.

Whenever Ajit was disappointed Sudha consoled him and said wait for tomorrow which could come with a renewed hope and vice-versa.

After a week, they both planned to visit Hyderabad which is considered to be a major hub for IT Industry. Most of the known names of industry had their presence in that city and there was a huge scope of business for Ajit & Sudha. They both took morning flight to Hyderabad with a renewed hope and optimism. Infact they met many clients and consultants throughout the day and were assured of a positive result. Incidentally there was no ego clash or awkward situation for Ajit like Pune as the people in this city are down to earth and comparatively honest in thoughts and actions. Sudha was happy and hopeful of some good results which was evident from her face, smile and body language.

In the evening after the good day's work reached airport for their return flight to MUMBAI. The flight was delayed for two hours so they both had plenty of leisure time in the airport lounge after security check-in etc. They both were sitting and discussing company affairs. The cupid in Ajit's mind and heart started acting and he was watching Sudha very closely, her eyes, lips and she herself totally as a woman.

Sudha was exceptionally beautiful and her beauty was not in the clothes, she was bearing, the figure, she carries or the way she styles her hair but the beauty of this female is seen in her eyes because that is the door way to her heart, the place where love resides. Her true beauty was reflecting in her soul. It is the caring attitude, the passions that she shows. The interesting part was that while Ajit was thinking lot of things about Sudha, she was not even knowing anything about him. She was innocently sitting, waiting for flight announcements.

Ajit thought to himself that everyone will tell you to never fish off the company pier. They are right as dating a company pier, co-worker is a touchy and potentially dangerous route. Understand that if something goes wrong, it may make things very awkward at work, even worse, you could even lose your job or career.

They also discussed lot of their personal problems related with office and home and finally sat in the aircraft at 10pm. Sudha was quite tired and was watching vacuum from window seat and Ajit was watching her profile and was hoping that Sudha's head will surely rest on his shoulder during the flight but all his hopes were dashed as she always maintained a safe distance between two bodies. Ajit was disappointed. They finally landed at 12 midnight and Ajit dropped her home and reached his residence well past midnight. He had a terrible night and was dilemma as to what to do? To convey or keep it to himself. Sudha was perceived differently by different people. She was sometimes adulterous and amorous lover and at others his consort. In Ajit's thoughts she was being accepted as a beloved of Ajit and wife of another.

CHAPTER 5

SIX MONTHS LATER

Ajit was stressed confused and in a state whether to convey or die with that desire of loving Sudha. Every moment he used to think she loves me or she doesn't only she knows. She has a child within. Ajit was a child even at 55 years and Sudha was merely 40 years. The gap was too wide. Ajit knows her but Sudha knows him better. Ajit expects her togetherness at all times. There is a soul between who is as dear as she is and cannot be neglected without a guilt. Guilt for what? It is unavoidable love with no feeling of flesh not even a feel of touch. He thought to himself "She loves him or not who cares? Atleast he loves her and will continue doing so till destiny creates a wall. Who cares?

At the same times, he rationally thinks, yes we have about 17 years of age gap, we also have mindsets of different generations. Do we have disagreements in our relationship? Of course they have, like any couple in healthy relationship. It is normal for people to disagree and even have arguments on occasions but they survive. They know the importance to learn from each other. They communicate because they love each other. He still had few misconceptions about his relationship with Sudha.

The first misconception in their relationship was that well he is an old guy, he can't possibly keep up pace with her. Their relationship is not going to work but Ajit thought that I might be older but I am still young at heart. I have heard Sudha telling people, he has got more energy than anyone she knows. There is a medical proof to say that she is right. A few years back when Ajit underwent some angioplasty his cardiologist said you have a heart of 25 years old youth now. Sudha used to ask Ajit, where do you get all that energy? From you only, was the instant reply from him. He used to tell Sudha that you are the source of my energy and they both started laughing on.

The second misconception about their relationship was that of sexual part of their relationship, must not be that great since he is much older. This is in case this relationship is taken to next level. Like most couples sex is an important part of any relationship. He feels that he has been loving this honeymoon for so many years now so this might not obstruct their relationship. Ajit was physically and sexually fit so the key to that part of relationship is summarily answered and he is blessed with an amazing lady. He thought to himself that she is not only a diamond, she is his God's answer to his prayers.

While Ajit's thoughts have reached that far Sudha was all ignorant about his feelings she only liked him as a responsible colleague. She used to like him a lot as a person who would surely take her out of woods and her company will come up. At times their eye contacts were giving both of them the pleasure of gaze. He was finding it extremely difficult to contain his feelings so one day, he decided to open up in front of Sudha, whatever were the consequences.

He was afraid of being rejected yes, he was also afraid of being accepted for wrong reasons.

Experience teaches you that every endeavour has 50-50 chances of failure or success regardless of your efforts. You might taste success in love but it need not be last. No need to blame love for that. Dou you want to get prosthetic feet, Ajit asked himself again and decided that he has to convey his feelings to Sudha irrespective of the consequences and went to office with firm determination. Sudha as usual was in office in dark blue Salwar Kameez with a fresh look. Her eye liner made her more beautiful and more inviting. Ajit wanted to say everything but developed cold feel. Long story short, there was a certain relationship of his which has been going on from six months and he was curious as to whether or not, this is love or just a relationship based on sympathy? Honestly if it is the second one, Ajit even didn't know if that's bad but he was sort of confused between sympathy and true love.

CHAPTER 6

AFTER ONE YEAR

Confusion continues since Ajit knew Sudha there could be most likely a mixture of the two happening. There were both sorts of feelings involved. But the thing about love is that it comes in various forms and levels. He thought that sympathy was part of love. When you love someone, you think about them a lot, you want to do anything to make them happy. A relationship takes a lot of work and if you are together for sympathy then that's not a very good relationship.

Ajit was fighting with his own self to determine whether to convey or let it be. Ajit was not a saint to contain his feelings and that adrenal rush, he was expressing within. He also thought "The desire to satisfy one's own senses is called lust while the desire to satisfy the senses of others like Sri Krishna, is called Prem, divine love of God and no matter what has happened, no matter what will be done he will always love her. He swears it. I am in love with you Sudha and I am not in habit of denying myself the simple pleasure of saying true things. I am in love with you and I know that love is just a shout into the void and that oblivion is inevitable. I know the second, I met you that there was something about you, I needed, it wasn't something about you. All it was just you and only you.

Remember, there is never a time or a place for true love. It happens accidently in nine heartbeats in a single flashing, throbbing moment. I don't care how hard being together is, nothing is worse than being apart. So much turmoil but Sudha was not aware of it. Now he attempted for the second time for the final assault.

In the meantime, Ajit got an offer for a job which was very lucrative and was similar to his position in his earlier company. As tragedy doesn't come alone, this offer made him think;

1) Can he get away from the feelings of Sudha which he is still not sure of maturity?

2) Will he also compensate for the loss of his ego, his insult from so many people who did this to him in this company because all those people will again beg for their flesh of work from Ajit?

3) Will he earn a big money over there as compared to present one?

4) Will he be happy to forget the promises he made to Sudha for bringing the company out of red?

After very carefully studying the balance sheet of above, Ajit decided to quit the job and leave the company and Sudha. Even though he had the guilt in him to prematurely leaving the company in mess but the feelings for Sudha were weighing more than anything. He thought that time is remedy for all sorrows and sufferings, he may also try to forget Sudha and Company. Anyway till now it was only one sided love and Sudha was not aware of the intensity and gravity of the situation except she used to love her being together in her cabin for hours together and also in the restaurants for meals or otherwise. He also thought that he will also reveal why he was intending to leave her and the company.

With utmost disgust but firm determination he asked Sudha if he could meet her in person as it was something very urgent. She nodded immediately and Ajit started explaining the purpose of his meeting her on such priority.

Look, Sudha, I have an offer from one of the biggest Real Estate Developer in Gurgaon as Head of Engineering Department where my financial package and status are pretty high. It is as good as my earlier assignment before joining this company. Secondly I am not sure whether you know that I have developed feelings of love and togetherness for you which is disturbing me and I am not able to justify my performance for the purpose, I have been appointed, I am disappointed.

She was taken for a rude shock as she never thought that a man of Ajit's stature and age will have these feelings for me. She must have concluded in her mind that he is just exploiting the situation like most of the people did and he thinks that I being a widow, would succumb to his advances. She composed herself and said, "Don't be disappointed.

Sometimes people need more time to make right or just decisions".

The news that Ajit was leaving that company spread like wild fire throughout the country. Before Sudha could even begin to ponder upon the consequences, she packed up her bag and left the office for solace.

While everyone around you might be thinking it is the time to move on or that you have finally begun to cope or normalize, you may be churning with turmoil and only beginning to understand the magnitude of what you have really lost. Sudha was in the same state of affairs and she wanted to be alone which is perfectly normal and acceptable.

Rather than looking at Sudha's behavior and trying to decide if it is normal compared to your feelings, are you in position to even imagine to leave? However difficult it may be, you must remind yourself that it is not about you. It is about her loss. Simply offering your own time and support can be most amazing gift and can help her on her road towards healing.

Ajit called her up in the evening to express his deep regrets for whatever happened during the day. Since he loved her so he wanted to make her life easy and for that whatever has to be done, he was prepared to do. Everything started off casual and they both continued chat till wee hours of the night. Ajit said, "At times he felt guilty as she was widow and for him it was hard to get her off his mind."

It was time when Sudha started bursting into anger and said, "what do you think Ajit, just because I have lost my husband and I was depending upon you for my company's survival, you have assumed that you can think, behave and speak whatever you want. I will let my company go to hell rather than even keeping your stay in my company as a bad dream.

Ajit, you can please take up your new assignment as and when you wish to and she cut the conversation abruptly. She was disturbed like anything. Both of them stopped talking for a month but it wasn't possible for both of them so they started off again with a just casual chat. Same old story again and again. Sudha confessed that she had some feelings for him but she could get over him soon. Again they were on and off for sometime.

Ajit never felt insulted or humiliated as he understood the mental agony and turmoil of Sudha but there were two important things in his mind that he will not leave Sudha with a broken heart and hope. He was not to satisfy his adrenaline rush as he had a firm belief that the desire as a reason for mating is the way of animals. He also knew that mistakes, failures, insult, frustration and rejections are part of progress and growth. Nobody ever achieved anything worthwhile without facing these five things.

With a clear thought in his mind he met Sudha and told her if one of us cries let both of us cry but preferably neither of us and further added that Sudha, let me be honest and confess to you today that from the moment I saw you few months ago, there has not been a single day that I have not waited for you. With every breath he has drawn, he has taken her name! For him the spring comes when he comes and meets her and winter begins when she is away from his sight. He feels that he lives in her.

He also confessed and said, "Sudha I am not totally mad at you, I'm just sad. You are locked up in that little world of yours and when I try knocking on the door, you just sort of look up for a second and go right back inside. I will not let it happen to you now. He could see some disappointment in her eyes but disappointment in romance may spell the end of the affair but it can also be beginning of real love. Sudha only responded that I do not know that what's the future of our this relationship but I admit your honesty and guts. That day the eyes contacts were pleasurable for both of them.

Ajit left that company and took up the new assignment. Though he was physically present in that company but his mind and soul were still with Sudha and he promised Sudha that he will come back after sometime and in between Ajit used to spend lot of time sitting in front of Sudha and talk for hours together.

It was an obvious truth that instant messaging has become the primary mode of communication between both of them and for many people specially for those involved in romantic relationship.

Both of them loved that feeling of being in love, the effect of having butterflies when you wake up in the morning that was special.

CHAPTER 7

FIRST OPEN DISCUSSION

It was Thursday, 3rd September Ajit got up after a disturbed sleep. It was quite frequent for him nowadays. There was nothing special. He went for a morning walk. The morning outside and at his jogging track was pleasant with few fitness freaks, walking and doing their workouts.

After a while they both (Ajit & Sudha) wished each other a pleasant good morning on What'sapp and a little later got another message from Sudha asking him to have lunch together either in 'HIMALAY KI GOAD MEIN OR SAGAR KI GAHARAIYON MEIN, two famous restaurants in Delhi suburbs. Ajit was excited to meet her with a hope that her emotions are taking exactly the same shape as he already has for her.

During the lunch, we both shared some secrets which were very very personal but it was only a trust and confidence we both shared with each other. As a matured and responsible person, she said. Ajit it is not that I do not care about you or not love you, may be the intensity is different. You are more vocal and I am not but yet you have become habit of my everyday life. But please understand, my situation is

100 percent different than your's. I have huge responsibility towards my family my kids, being a single mother. I can't afford to be known as somebody whose husband has expired few months back has affair that too with her own colleague.

Ajit would never try to understand what Sudha wanted. All she wanted to limit his emotions and not make it too obvious so that the whole would will look into it with a suspicious mind. Ajit tried his best to explain to her that except emotions and feelings he knows his limits and would never cross them. Sudha held his hand to reassure him that she also loves him but certain social and other compulsions are stopping her to move even one inch beyond a very respectable relationship.

Ajit was mad and would not agree to her. He would understand and would agree with her on all issues but he would never leave Sudha and degree of his possessiveness for Sudha was beyond limits. Both enjoyed each other's company in the restaurant till they were actually forced to leave the place because the eatery gets closed at 4pm. Both returned to their office and still continued in the corridor for a while. The day ended as usual partially official discharge and partially sorting out the internal conflict within.

At about 9pm, Sudha called up. Ajit as usual was excited to talk to her. For few moments the conversation was normal the same explanation and same denial by Ajit.

Ajit felt that today Sudha's voice seems to be partially choked as she said Ajit your emotions have started disturbing me and I feel a bit insecure for my kids, my self-respect and also the social stigma. Today even my very close friend also passed sarcastic comment like Sudha, you have become so busy with Ajit that you do not have time to talk to me. Sudha also told that even our staff looks at her suggesting and confirming our relationship without speaking and it may be a serious problem for both of us to run the company.

Your emotions are increasing and suggesting next level which I cannot afford. I reiterate that I love you but I cannot make and accept it in public due to non-compatibility between both of us. Age is the biggest hurdle otherwise situation would have been different.

Ajit thought for a while, went into pensive mood and thought "love is to give and not to take". Let me forget my selfish motto and sacrifice all emotions for a person whom he loves to core of his heart and confirmed that from tomorrow onwards Ajit is going to improve, no expression of emotions, cut down on Whatsapp messages. It was a difficult choice but for her sake anything anytime, anywhere and at any cost. Ajit deleted 2192 Whatsapp messages. Ajit was not sure of his resolutions but as a true Singh, he would respect and be devoted and committed without even she knowing it.

Next day till 10pm, all was normal, a bit unusual gloomy and serious but let him see what happens next. The night was terrible, slept on and off and finally got up at 4:52am. Ajit himself you have made your life miserable and also making Sudha's life even worse. She is already affected by her personal tragedy with a huge responsibility.

She still loves you with an intensity you cannot measure. The only difference you can express and she has to contain within. Your answer that inspite of your best efforts, you cannot stop loving her, seems to be selfish. Why don't you suffer instead of that innocent, dignified lady? You will have to answer yourself, someday which may be too late to rectify. Atleast continue trying for it but under no circumstances, you will express it to become a story in public. You have already become a Casanova in the eyes of her few friends. All the best guy.

Sudha could never see anybody unappy as she is a very kind hearted soft hearted female so may be she must have felt a bit of uneasy on part of Ajit's plight. There was some fire within her for Ajit and it was like melting of ice.

She did not know how old was he until six months into their this so called relationship, he had applied for a job and Sudha took a sneaky look at his C.V., Bio-data. How would it be, she pondered if he was just 10 years or so older than I am. Of course I would still find him attractive but would things have worked out to be same?

While his achievements are laudable what caught her eye is how he is getting hotter even as he gets older. He looks smoulding hot when he is mid 5th decade of his life. Looking around she discovered lot about that man who not only carries his age very well but his sex appeal too has gone up a few notches than he was younger.

Ajit loved that helping out with a good cause brought them together. They both continued to contribute to the organization. They booked few good jobs in Pune, Hyderabad, Bengaluru and MUMBAI. They both admitted that supporting a good deed/ charity has always paid off for them.

Chapter 8

AFTER 15 MONTHS

As expected Ajit rejoined the company as there was an unwritten understanding between them that nobody will take his place and as usual they started together in the company affairs on day to day basis. Sudha was business savvy and he was to go with it. They both started going to their project sites, meetings and were mostly for lunch together and they in the process explored few best of the restaurants in Delhi. They visited MINI PUNJAB, DELHI DURBAR, PANCHAVATI & ROYAL CHALLENGE and Sudha used to comment that the menu you order is always good and to my taste. Generally you have a good taste. Yes, Ajit winked at her and said that you are also one of them which now she used to consume and not retort.

Normally if you tame a dog at home, you start loving it whereas Ajit was a good human being, man with a presentable attitude and personality and this exercise was practically bringing them a bit more closer. Once Ajit offered her Vodka with orange juice which she liked though she did not finish the drink.

Whether they were sitting in office or in a restaurant, they used to love their togetherness. Ajit says, "There was something unique in her eyes which according to him was that Ajit could see through hours, days and months together.

Ajit stared deep into her eyes and said I have to avoid looking at your face and eyes as much as possible because when he does it, all he wants to do is kiss and also gaze at the sty under her left eye. So you noticed that also asked Sudha. Can you stop looking at me now and concentrate on your work, we are in the office, No but Ok. He was left with no option but to go to his cabin as a disappointed gambler. Anyway disappointments are to the soul what thunderstorms are to air. However day ended and were back home respectively.

Next day they left for a Clients meeting. Sudha did not have a driver that day and Ajit never wanted a driver so to his good luck, she said she would drive Ajit to the meeting place. Both of them took the Car from the basement and she sat on the driver's seat and Ajit to her left. I do not know why Sudha was in a good and in a bit romantic mood, Ajit asked himself and Sudha said that she wants to hug Ajit. What does a blind man need, eyes, so was Ajit, she hugged Ajit and Ajit very gently kissed her in the Car. Trust me, it was divine, they both said and now sparks were sure to fly. She developed trust on him and Ajit developed taste for that. She also put her hand on Ajit's shoulder. Do not put your hand on my shoulder, he said as her touch sends waves down the back of his neck. What do you want? the next question Sudha asked. Ajit wants to be a couple, as he is not a teenager to joke around. His voice was firm and defiant.

Ajit became more vocal to Sudha, he said first love is unforgettable moment in somebody's life. He also felt the same and he wanted to protect Sudha from every bad things. He said to her that this feeling will never fade. As long as you are in my life, my heart, my mind, my soul, my spirit, you will remain.

Ajit had to go away from her for a month for some of his family's unavoidable functions in Mumbai and for almost a month, they both remained unmet and also their conversation was limited due to serious communication signal problems in the deep mountains. So they just used to talk more business than romance. Their relationship for this period was of a special type known as 'PARAKRIYA RASA or UNWEDDED LOVE. Even from our mundane experience, we know that such relationship can be of greater intensity than within marriage. Ajit knew that when a woman's beloved is away, she thinks of him more than he is present before her.

He came back and met Sudha after a formal Hi & How have you been, how was your trip etc. etc.? Ajit asked her tell me with conviction whether you love me and AD-RIB came from Sudha. No, I do not really know whether I love you or not but yes, you have become the habit of my daily life. I need time, I would like to see the future of our relationship. Can we take it to next level specially when there are serious issues of compatibility of age and you are married with a most respected family. I would certainly not ruin somebody's life and get cursed. She confessed that even though she has immense love and feelings of a woman to be shared with you but you know the situation where I cannot think of the second level with you.

You are the man, I have been fantacising for quite some time but it looks that certain things possibly cannot be done. Ajit agreed with Sudha and told Sudha, I agree with you not that I have not thought it over and again but I think I have gone beyond ethics, morality of whatever you want to say. I promise that my this relationship with you will never adversely affect my family except a guilt in mind but probably my heart has overruled my mind and you have become something, I imagine, think, talk, care or worship.

Sudha was not satisfied by the assurance. "Will you always remember me? They for the first time involved in a passionate kiss. After a while, Sudha got up and began to tie her disheveled tresses into a knot and asked Ajit once again, "Will we always be together? Ajit replied that they were inseparable. You will always be my princess but nothing will hold me from my destiny and my duty.

CHAPTER 9

AFTER SIXTEEN MONTHS

They both pledged that whatever may be the consequences of this relationship, each one of us will share their happiness, sadness, secrets and have to work as one mind in two bodies. Sudha, as a consequent to this very hesitantly said, Ajit I was feeling very uneasy for not informing you that I have registered myself with one of the matrimonial sites last week. You know I never wanted to involve in such things as I have enough of my problems in office as well as on domestic fronts. But my family and friends specially my Bhabhi, have insisted on getting it done as according to them it is very difficult to survive the cruelty of this society in absence of a man that also according to them, I am too young and single.

It was a rocking shock to Ajit but he also analytically agreed for her this arrangement. Even though hell broke out on Ajit's sentiments by the basic idea of Sudha leaving her some day. Ajit thought absolutely on logical grounds and told Sudha, I respect your decision but probably you will have to understand that it is difficult for most of the people to accept you with two children, secondly most of the people will either be widowed or divorcees or never married for reasons, thirdly most of the people on such sites are perverts and just like to have fun. I would only request you to share each and every information of such applicants so that atleast I can give you my input. Trust me all the advice will be impartial. Jokingly she said, Are you going to do my 'Kanyadan' or what? Certainly not I am not a saint but yes, I will like to do 'Kanyadan' of your daughter. She smiled with a trust. Ajit asked what sort of man I should keep in mind, what are your specifications?

She said that she had this image of a perfect man, well settled, good looking, matured and a person who could treat her as a kid and anybody like Ajit if he would not have been married, an emotional and concerned about my kids. When the search started it was like what could have been a needle in a hay stack.

See the trust and love she had for Ajit, she shared her e-mail ID and password for all such matrimonial transactions. She once trusted Ajit upto the extent that described TRUST – Giving someone authority to destroy you completely, but having the confidence that he would never do it!!

CHAPTER 10

AFTER 20 MONTHS

Ajit sometimes used to visit Sudha's home also and was quite friendly with both of her kids and discussed about their studies, interests etc. and also used to part with certain useful tips for their studies and sports activities. He was also liked by her both parents and her friends but nobody even smelt an iota of our about our relationship except, they all knew that Ajit is helping her in running her business as a colleague.

Once such day Ajit visited Sudha's residence to pick her up as her driver did not turn up. She opened the door for him. She had just come out of the washroom after her bath. She was not fully dressed up and her hair were wet and face very cute and beautiful, a perfect radiance.

The cupid in Ajit, was increasing the rush of blood in his nerves. Nor did his romance fulfill his deepest desires, not content with this mere friendly relationship, Ajit was searching for the ideal union of body and soul that has escaped him in his earlier marriage. He embraced this quest with passion and an urgency. Sudha, was not a super woman and she also had desires to satisfy. He felt that everything, he did, every touch, every caress, every physical pleasure, she gave was divine. If she touched him so he would die and then the thought crawled into his brains that if she did not touch him then also he would die. The same was applicable to Sudha in letter and spirit.

After she sat against him, her hair tickling his face. He wanted Sudha to melt in him like butter on toast. He wanted to absorb her and walk around for rest of her life. Sudha with her eyes closed said, everywhere you touch me, was a fire, my whole body is burning up and two of us are becoming twin points of same bright white flame. They did not blame each other for this but Sudha never came to office that day.

Ajit one day visited Sudha's home and met her children daughter 13 years and son 9 years and asked them what they would like to be come in future. The girl opted for medicine and the boy a technocrat. Ajit explained the daughter in Sanskrit "Udhyamane Hi Sidhanti Karyani na manorathai, Nahi Suptasya Singhast Pravishante Mukhe Mraga" which means everything can be achieved with hard work and not by simply wanting it. Like a deer will not enter in a lion's mouth without lion chasing for it. Remember this is guru mantra for you to achieve everything in life.

To the boy, also as he was mother's pet, his everything ends with mother so Ajit told him in Sanskrit too.

"Kak Chestha Bako Dhyanam, Swan Nidra Tathaivcha, Alpahari Grihatyagi, Vidhyarthi Panch Lakshyadam" which means you should have an attempt to do things, like a crow and your concentration should be like Bagula (ANDEOLA GRAII), you call them Bagula Bhagat, your sleep should be like that of dog, not of Kumbhakaran, you should be a less eater, should not have much thinking of home every time. These are the 5 symptoms of a good students. You will always remember me for these words of advice.

They were quite friendly with Ajit. Sometimes Ajit used to tell Sudha that in case we become couple, atleast your daughter will adopt me. Your son is too small to say anything. Get out of the world of dreams, Ajit. If it is not possible, it is not possible.

CHAPTER 11

Sudha discussed two cases of matrimonial proposals. One was an established software professional 45 years old, from down south having his own business of overseas recruitment of software engineers. He was quite good looking and he seemed to be acceptable based on the details available on the site. Ajit also checked his details on Google and Linked-in portals and told Sudha, that you can communicate your acceptance to proceed further and open the chat with that man. She started chatting with him and Sudha upto some large extent, got interested in him. For Ajit, though it was a difficult moment, but with a very heavy heart and also with a sense of duty, was helping her to know the man properly. He advised Sudha to get clarification on following issues;

1) Whether the kids are acceptable to him?

2) Whether he would relocate himself from Chennai to Delhi.

The answer came almost immediately that he only wanted a live in type relationship and both the things are not acceptable. Sudha was advised to forget about this proposal as she can't afford to compromise on any of this issues. Though Sudha was inclined for her likes but left the proposal for larger interests, Ajit very categorically told her that your priorities are kids and your company so Ajit will not feel happy if you even continued chatting with that South Indian Punjabi.

Second case was a 40 years youth from Pune, middle class Sales person in some Pharmaceutical company. Sudha met him couple of times, and was good looking, simple habits, soft spoken and was accepting whatever Sudha was asking him to accept. He was also fitting in the parameters but according to Sudha, he was having an inferiority complex like he is a Sales Manager and Sudha is the owner of a company. Ajit only asked if a guy is so good looking, smart, employed, why is he accepting each and everything. The fact came out that his divorce has not come through and the reason, he gave for divorce was that his earlier wife, a Punjabi girl was too demanding and autocratic. Sudha could also be demanding so he would divorce again or what. This guy after two meetings, just left a SMS that let us just be good friends as it may not be possible to take it to the next level.

Ajit told Sudha that even though my personal motive is involved as I might lose you but I will give you absolutely impartial and correct advice, I will never leave you with someone who can make your life worse. I will not feel happy if anything like this happens with you. The best is that you do not get married until an exceptional proposal comes. I am there for everything, a woman needs in life and also I will be there even if you settle down in life with the same intensity of love and responsibility. That means, you want that I should have extra marital affairs with you even after I get married, Sudha asked smilingly and jokingly to which Ajit said, Yes.

Excess of everything is bad including love. It hurts even on minor utterances, misunderstandings. In addition to their togetherness in work, they were together from 11:30pm to 3:00am on instant messages i.e. Whatsapp etc. and it had become their habit and primary mode of communication and there was not even a single day, they have not waited for each other. You can fix up & set timings of watch to make it 23:30 hours when instant message saying Hi, came. She used to tell Ajit almost always that see my destiny, now I cannot marry a person who now fits in all my requirements like run my company, care about my children and loves me too. May be next birth I/we might do it. Everyday this discussion was continuing till 3:30am, as both loved signing to each other on those odd hours. Ajit used to sing – 'Ham Tere Pyar Mein Saara Aalam Kho Baithe' and Sudha – 'Ye Kahan Aa Gaye Ham, Tere Saath Chalte Chalte'.

They both felt bad if one of them was not able to chat for even valid reasons and lot of explanation was required to satisfy them.

CHAPTER 12

Their love was blossoming and infact it was on rising curve day by day. On the other hand Commercial market was going down. No of jobs were not increasing and business for everyone including them was not good. The payment from the Clients was not coming though whereas the payment to vendors, was playing havoc with them and they both were under severe financial stress. Ajit was having some surplus money from his last employment, so he offered to come out of the crisis of non-payments. She would agree for everything under the Sun, but accepting financial support from Ajit. Her simple argument was that if she accepted financial help from him, she would find it easy escape and would not strive to earn from the projects, they are doing. She was stubborn and would take the shit from vendors, sub-contractors but would not opt for the means, suggested by Ajit.

They would sit together, discuss the prevailing financial situations in lunch break and eat home cooked food from Sudha's kitchen. At times she used to bring 'Baigan ka Bhurta' and Russian Salad in her tiffin box which Ajit used to like too much. She also used to comment on Ajit saying that you are the only person who eats apples with skin peeled off. Whenever she was in a good mood, she used to speak MUMBO-JUMBO, a language that sounds mysterious but has no real meaning.

CHAPTER 13

STRUGGLE CONTINUES..............

When you are in position to give something to somebody, they are prepared to bow down to kneel to you upto any extent but the moment, you go to a situation when you have to take something from them or from anybody, they expect you to bow down deeper than them. This was constantly happening to Ajit. At times, he used to think why was he begging and did he deserve this treatment?

Nobody bothered to even think that Ajit never wanted anything for himself. All he wanted, was for the company, he was working for and owned by Sudha and that also in exchange of good service, good product at a reasonable cost. This made him a bit irritated with the system and he took it to his mind and body and a surge of anger ran through his entire body.

Clearly a work environment that includes insults, belittling, can erode and employee's morale. What is less understood is that such a toxic work atmosphere, can lead to deteriorating health. Feeling trapped continuously in such working conditions, can actually have risk of heart disease. This is what happened to Ajit. So long as this stress was within comfort zone, he performed better under pressure and motivated him to do the best but when the stress became overwhelming it damaged his health, mood and productivity and also his relationship and quality of life.

Mounting of payments, reduction of jobs in the market and insulting out bursts of Clients and vendors made him a sick man. He still struggled but when the repeated experiences, the fight of stress in his daily life, it raised his blood pressure, suppressed the immune system, increased the risk of heart attack and stroke, speeded up his aging process and left him vulnerable to host of mental and emotional problems. He finally landed up in a hospital for treatment and it was detected that his stress levels were very high for following reasons:-

1) Chronic worry

2) Pessimism

3) Negative self talk

4) Unrealistic expectations

5) Lack of flexibility

Needless to mention that Ajit had already undergone Angioplasty 7 years back.

Ajit was having a little sensation of heavy chest, slight pain in both jaws and both the hands. He was not comfortable. He was shifted to ICU No.3 and was lying on the bed. He was able to occasionally see the doctor and very occasionally Sudha. His private clothes were removed and he was given a Kurta and Pyzama from the hospital. He was not aware of hospital formalities like fee etc. which Sudha did manage somehow.

It was decided by the panel of doctors and Sudha to carryout Angiography and Angioplasty if needed. They all gave him the first major indication that all is not well with his life and finally taken on a patient's trolley to the operation theatre. Ajit says that when he was being shifted from ICU room to OT, he had time to remember to Shiva, Ram and Maa Durga and after remembering Gods, he started sinking into thoughts, questions but no answers;

1) Whether he would come back alive

2) He did not talk to Sudha

3) He did not explain to do what at home and office in case something happens to him

There was a glass partition between OT and viewers gallery so I could atleast see that they all were assuring me of all good. Angiography was done and it was found that there is a heavy deposition of some unwanted stuff in one of the main artery was found to be 90% blocked and finally angioplasty was done successfully and was brought back to ICU room. Ajit spent 9 days in that hospital and came back home. The experience of this entire episode was good as Ajit was drawn closer to Sudha. She must have lost approx.. 5 Kg of weight, making her 58 Kg. He told her that my illness made you fit. She only smiled and no words came out of her mouth. This was good indication for Ajit to understand that it is not necessary to repeat 'I Love You, I Love You but to feel. Ajit was advised one month's complete bed rest.

CHAPTER 14

Ajit resumed after 45 days and was briefed by Sudha what he was not aware of during last approximately two months. They both started with new energy and with the feeling that they will and in some time they will become a force to reckon within the industry. The message was very clear, "If you have never failed, you have not lived" and they decided to believe, thinking that everyone that succeeds, has had nothing but luck all their life and they had it easy, is only a myth and we forget that for that success there was a long hard struggle to get there.

Ajit was repeatedly telling Sudha that he has witnessed this count number of times. The people that succeeded were the people, who weren't afraid of rejections. Sales is all about rejection and for some people, the risk of being rejected was so paralyzing that they would not approach a potential Client. The result – No Sales No success.

With this determination they both entered the market and started meeting same people who were once not supportive. The same guys this time had a different attitude and body language and started giving them jobs. Ajit on the other hand also ventured out into different business segments like Textiles, Pharma industries so on so forth. Why deny

51

yourself the opportunity to accomplish everything that you ever wanted of life. This was the key that unlocked the door to your dreams. Your success is directly proportional to the number of times you fail which is also directly proportional to the number of times you try.

Hard work never fails, they had a target of Rs.50 Crores business and they were able to achieve Rs.36 Crores in that financial year.

CHAPTER 15

AFTER 4 YEARS

They were happy living and loving the creative dream of life with a full time business of their own. Being the Boss, there was no pressure of time as the work came to them automatically and they didn't go to the market every day. Then that all started late November, when the work load started drying up. By early March next year, their front door no longer, resembled a revolving door. It was more like a steel gate locking people out. Calling for help Ajit found himself leaning on business associate and those big companies but thinking their business going to collapse in a few short months, they both began to panic. The consultants and the clients, all doubted his ability and business experience. Losing confidence even in his abilities, Ajit even thought that may be people didn't like him. The 'decline' in business not only disturbed Ajit but Sudha also. She was not only mentally disturbed but financially also. The same old story of non-payments and exceptional pressure from vendors and sub-contractors. There were few Clients and Consultants whom Ajit never wanted to meet as their attitude towards Ajit was same old one and it hurt his self-respect and ego. While the same was communicated to Sudha, she did not take it too kindly as she used to be years back even supporting unconditionally. May be, she has acquired confidence on herself and she told Ajit, Ajit Ok, you don't meet him, I will meet them and went upto the extent of telling Ajit that she will appoint somebody to look after Sales & Marketing and Ajit will look after all technical and commercial part of the business operations. This was the first thin line drawn between both of them. In any case, even Ajit wanted Sudha to be little independent as she was depending 100%, even for petty issues. Ajit partially withdrew from the scene for such sales issues. Sudha, basically is a sharp and intelligent female, so she understood the indifference from Ajit and wanted to discuss all these threads of disharmony in business and our deep rooted relationship.

CHAPTER 16

It was a bright sunny morning, cool breeze indicating an early winter, was blowing. Ajit was busy in his morning walk which was a regular feature of his daily routine. In fact this morning was more beautiful after few cloudy and dark days. His walk was interrupted by an early morning telephone call from Sudha. Hi, are you busy in something urgent or calls? I just want to speak to you for a moment. Her voice was so sweet that Ajit wanted to say that you have made my day but she sounded a bit composed so he withdrew and said, Yes, please go ahead. Could you please come over to my place today? I have to share and discuss something very immediate, you can make it any time during the day.

Ajit was curious and nervous of this invitation and was also sure of that Sudha had something which she needs solved immediately otherwise normally she wouldn't have called so early. Ajit prepared himself as if he is going on his first date, nice dress, soothing perfume (Normally he doesn't use even after shave lotion) and reached at her place at 9:30am sharp. Sudha was as usual getting ready to go to office and was in a silk light coloured gown with wet hair and her face showed radiance filled with beauty. She did not appear to be that disturbed as Ajit thought so. She offered nice hot tea and some cookies. She also asked if Ajit wanted those typical Punjabi Parathas which he declined.

Ajit asked Sudha what was the matter and why were you sounding panicky and worried? She said, Yes I was worried not for myself or business but was worried about both the kids and I needed a man to advise them as they respect you and listen to you so I had no option but to rely on you. My daughter wants to go for Arts in graduation where I want her to go for medicines and she is not prepared to heed my advice. She wants to pursue IAS after graduation and I want her to become a doctor. There is a serious conflict between mother and daughter. I remember that you once advised her to concentrate on Science, she religiously followed that and probably she would listen to you for sure now also.

Similarly my son wants to go for Mass Media and I want him to become an engineer. After all, he has to take care of our company 'some day'. Both the jobs were more difficult for Ajit as he could manage to design a space ship but changing the direction of two kids, were herculean task, thought for some time and asked Sudha, where are the kids? Gone to school, was instant reply from Sudha, let me think it over, I do not guarantee that they will follow what you want but yes for sure, I will ensure that they follow the right education. Do you trust me? Blindly she said and asked for some time to plan and talk to both the kids separately.

Ajit wanted to leave her house but Sudha's last few words stopped him and was carried away in thoughts beyond his imaginations. She said that Ajit after sharing my these issues, I somehow feel that you have taken somebody's place in my life and I do not bother much for their education, career etc. in life and frankly speaking I do not miss him now. It is almost 6 years after his demise and almost 5 years with you. Ajit did not actually understand the meaning of this conversation whether what she had said is, just a slip of tongue or did she really mean what she said. He was numb for some time and before he could regain his normal sense, he noticed a mischievous smile on Sudha's face. She said don't read between lines. I have a very strong liking for you and strong sense of confidence.

As such Ajit used to be timid specially after seeing deep in her eyes. Her eyes were his weakness and an invitations to go closer.

Ajit could remember it like it happened just yesterday. The passion and the fire, he had felt when it happened, was something he can't describe in words. He describes, "we had just entered the bed room and it was our second moment together. We spent a lot of time together but never crossed the line as they believed in their religion." Ajit was restless, wondering how would he react when Sudha would touch him.

The bed room smelt divine like rose petals were sprinkled everywhere. It was entirely romantic and the fragrance of Sudha ignited his senses. The ambience of the room with beautiful silk curtains was magnificent and they both could see the view of half the city from her top floor apartment. Ajit put his hand around Sudha's waist and kissed her neck. It was electrifying as they never experienced anything like it before.

Are you enjoying the view Sudha asked Ajit, yeah, it is romantic as you are. I have been waiting for this from a long time too, Ajit said.

Sudha sensed him inhale sharply as he started pulling her closer to him and his lips lightly brushed Sudha's and they both felt a current pass though them. Ajit switched off the lights and lit few candles. Sudha sat on the bed shuffling her silk gown staring at the man who looked breath taking in his tuxedo. He towered over her but mannerisms made him like a gentle handsome giant. Sudha never wanted to disappoint the man so she was perfect and co-operative in every way. Without wasting another second his lips crashed on her's. It felt like a dam had burst releasing all his energy that was held in. They both have gone for it and all said about religion vanished like a straw in a thunderstorm.

When they realized what has happened, was too late and though they both admitted for a guilt but you can't reverse the direction of flow of river.

CHAPTER 17

A WEEK LATER

After a week, Ajit took Sudha's kids for lunch in a nearby restaurant. Sudha excused herself pretending to be busy in an unavoidable meeting but the fact of the matter was that Ajit wanted only the kids for some serious discussion and counselling. Ajit ordered some nice Chicken Tikka and Paneer Chilly as both the kids loved that. He also ordered some Pinacolada virgin for both of them and a simple tomato soup for himself. The teenagers were happy and excited as they could order anything, speak anything as the Mom was not there and Ajit wanted them attuned to understand what is wrong or right for both of them for their professional career in future. Now since you are appearing for your 12th Standard in couple of months, what is going to be your aim? Asked Ajit and Prachee like her mother said I have not finally decided but I have an aptitude to become an administrator. I will try for an IAS position. There is lot of hard work involved in it Prachee, why don't you opt for medicines and become a Doctor? You will look beautiful and dignified after wearing that Doctor's white coat.

I hope Mumma has not asked you to make me understand? There is more hard work in medicines study than IAS preparations, secondly I have no interest in pursuing this field as it is not only MBBS, you have to do Masters and then specialization. By the time I do all this, I will become old. Don't you think, I am talking sense Uncle?

I appreciate your time of thought and would support you. Yes, your Mom told me to convince you for medicines but now you have convinced me so go ahead and I will be with you all the time.

Now, it is your turn prince Ishan, since you also have to plan your Xth Board so you will have to plan your line of career in XIth, Engineering, Medicines, Chartered Accountancy, Law or what? Ishan is very innocent and without understanding much of the depth of the subject told Ajit that he would like to go for Mass Media of Films, Agreed, you are sharp, good looking and can surely succeed in these areas but these areas are a bit risky, everyone cannot become ARNAV GOSWAMY or SALMAN so struggle is too big. Will you be able to face all these problems? Ajit asked. Why don't you try to become a successful Mechanical Engineer and develop something of your own and you can also take care of the business which your Mom is taking care. You could relieve her and take your company in the next orbit. I know that you being sincere, you will be successful in this endeavor. Prince thought very seriously for some time and agreed as advised by Ajit. They left the restaurant on happy note. Ajit felt happy and assured that he has done his job properly and talked to Sudha that she should support Prachee to go for Arts specially English Literature, Political Science and

Sociology and encourage her for his choice of career. For Prince she was happy that Ajit has made him understand. She thanked Ajit from the core of her heart and hugged him so tightly that Ajit had to respond same way.

CHAPTER 18

Meanwhile there were two new proposals sent by some marriage portals. Sudha wanted to discuss with Ajit. Ajit wondered himself that he loves Sudha and Sudha wants his opinion on this issue. Funny was the situation with him. But he had promised her that he would help her settle down in life, if the proposal is genuine and meets all specifications laid down by Ajit to Sudha. There was one from Rajesh Kumar, 45 years, 5'7" divorcee, no children, Hindu Punjabi, Masters in Finance, staying in Faridabad, ready to relocate to MUMBAI. He is good looking and earning Rs.15 Lacs to 20 Lacs annually. Another was Mahendra Singh, 44 years, 5'11", divorcee, clean shaven Jat Sikh settled in Canada. He says that he is sincere about finding a right woman and settle down in life. He is prepared to give unconditional love and care. He has two kids staying with his ex-wife.

Ajit said, "Remarriages are more complicated and at risk than the first marriage. Yes it is also correct that they need the same strong and consistent nurturing as first one, no matter what yours stage of life or circumstances. Family life with children is one of the most stressful times in any marriage due to the never ending physical demands.

Why do you want to get married again at 45 years? Is it the fear of your becoming weak physically due to ageing or do you want to become a parasite? Nothing like that Ajit but family pressure keeps the thought of marriage live in my mind.

The most important thing as I told you few years back is to take your kids in confidence. They are both teenagers now and understand things much better. Will they accept somebody more close to you then they themselves? Have you judged and known the honesty of the people.

Think ten times as this decision of yours is, going to change life for you, for kids, for your business drastically.

My advice to you, will be negative, though it may sound like a bit selfish but at the same time I am concerned about you and kids and would not be in a position to bear anything adverse in your life.

I am a woman too, she retorted. So you have a man though libido is going down with respect to time but even you are also not 20 or 30 years old. So it is Ok. Ajit answered in the same fashion as Sudha commented and asked. Ok, the idea of remarriage will not come in our way from today onwards. However if there is anybody as honest as loving, as caring as Ajit, he would agree, he promised. Sudha said, No not now or probably never.

CHAPTER 19

AN YEAR LATER

The phase of slowdown in market started and the business in their company, started bearing the brunt of situations. It is common to operate the business in loss especially if it is still finding its feet. If you are operating at a loss it means the total taxes deductible, expenditure of business, are greater than its income for the financial year. If a business continues to operate at a loss and don't change course, it will inevitably fail. If the business is frequently operating at loss because you are in a consistent period of slow sales, it is advisable to seek expert advice and consult a tax advisor to help you to turn things around. This situation of loss continued for 3 to 4 years and the company still continued to work with the hope that it will be profitable in the future and if it was true than there is no limit on number of years and would survive on nett business losses.

All that the company needed then was;

1) Business Plan

2) Some realistic expectation of being profitable in the future

3) To maintain all records to make decisions and report income

4) Carryout the activities in a business like manner

5) Change your methods of operations in an attempt to improve profitability

6) Make profit from the appreciation of the company assets

7) Start selling your product at a loss to remain in business

8) Look into your manpower cost to avoid make organization top heavy

9) Avoid disharmony at work place as it can be an unfortunate fact of life and for the health of the company. To avoid disharmony at work place, take following corrective actions;

   i) Improve drastically on poor communication and consultations

   ii) Avoid short vision and have shared vision

   iii) Avoid mistrust leading to interpersonal conflict

   iv) Have proper and justified leadership

With the above advice to Sudha, Ajit was frank enough to even convey that even if some outside expertise is needed, it should be done on war footings. You may see my struggle but you will never see me quit. I am not a perfect person, I make lot of mistakes but I really appreciate those people who stay with us after knowing how I really am, Ajit told Sudha. Sudha consulted some close people to her and started looking out for the outside support. Some of the people from her inner courtyard, even advised to sell the company.

The process of selling the company or running it by some other company on profit sharing basis was initiated. Since the financial results of company from last few years, were not encouraging, so the offers from the market were either very low priced or on no loss no profit basis.

Many companies requested for balance sheets of last three years to assess and quote their price for take over. Even though Sudha was consulting Ajit on each and every step but was more influenced by the so called close people of the inner courtyard. Finally an offer from East India came which briefly was as under.

They would operate the company with Sudha and run it for two years. In these two years they will pay off all the liabilities of banks, taxes of all statutory bodies and pay a lumpsum after two years. Even if the company doesn't earn profit in two years, they both will jointly find the customer and take it to logical end. An agreement was signed between Sudha and that East Indian company. Ajit told Sudha that he would be helping her from outside but would not work as an employee under the new management. In fact the new

Directors were also not comfortable with Ajit as Ajit was a very senior person in the industry and probably they were not in position to advise Ajit on any matters. Ajit left that company after this arrangement.

CHAPTER 20

SIX MOTNTHS LATER........

The partnership was not comfortable as the alliance didn't produce any positive results either in turns of business development or in terms of generating profitability. In fact the partners were not even acceptable in the market. The main partner was simply using this office to generate and increase their other business. Sometimes the owners of the business whether that business be partnership, a limited company or a limited liability partnership, fall into dispute. The dispute might for example be about the way the business is run or the way profits are shared. Any dispute within a business quietly causes damage and it is vital to resolve these disputes.

The new partners must have thought that Sudha's company might prove to be a gold mine and they would reap the fruits without investing much in form of finance and labour. They gave Sudha a feeling that they somehow want to opt out of the understanding. Partners or Directors who are intent on leaving the partnership or company Directorship are more dangerous to remain.

The biggest challenge in front of Sudha was to deal with a non-performing business partner because a business cannot succeed without good working relationship between its partners or shareholders. If the relationship breaks down, the consequences can be devastating.

Since the company was not doing well and the relationship was at the brink of breakdown, Sudha only thought to relieve them whatever may be consequences. She remembered the words Ajit said once before entering into agreement with these people. Try to understand people before trusting them. Because we are living in such a world where artificial lemon flavour is used for welcome drinks and real lemon is used in finger bowl. If at any point of time if you feel that your existence is in a danger of terminal damage, I suggest you do some hard thinking instead of hard chasing. Sudha did exactly same and said bye bye to that East Indian company.

Ajit was not with her in this moment. She called him in the evening and said that I am a free bird now and now I have to survive at my own from today. Do you hear me Ajit?

Subsequently Sudha got many proposals like somebody told her that he would manage his company and take it out of red and his stake will be his sweat money but will partner for 50% shares.

Some said that they will run the company and once it is in profit, they would expect 50% profit.

Meanwhile Sudha was more or less forced to employ Shetty, a close friend of Sudha's trustworthy, family friends. Shetty was having knowledge of administration and legal affairs whereas his knowledge in the field of company business was more or less NIL. Any way to take care of statutory requirements of banking and taxation, Sudha appointed him. Ajit was not in agreement with this appointment as the need of the hour was to appoint a technocrat, to be known as the face of the company but his advice was overruled and he kept quiet.

CHAPTER 21

TWO YEARS LATER

In 12th, Ishan demonstrated a higher level of competence in Mathematics & Science and also did reasonably well in English. Ajit thought that this was the right moment to advise him for Engineering Degree and that too in Computer Science and Application or Mechanical Engineering and also shared with him what course, colleges, he is expected to see. Ajit also encouraged him to take most rigorous and challenging courses for his academic level. He was admitted in coaching classes for Engineering admission in IITs or NITs. He took keen interest and promised Ajit that he will seriously pursue his advice. It was his hard work and good fortune that he got admission in IIT Kharagpur. Ajit was overjoyed and so was Sudha. All arrangements were made to send him far away.

Since Ishan was a bit timid and of shy nature, Ajit ensured and explained to him everything how he has to face all challenges of college and hostel ragging etc. and be responsible for himself as there is no Ajit Uncle and no Mom. He joined the degree course and settled in hostel with few problems of ragging etc. which he handled nicely. May be a bit difficult but manageable. After two months, he was comfortable and used to the new environment, new friends. Ishan was very particular to keep his mother and Ajit informed of everything. This is how time flies, after four years Ishan became a graduate in Mechanical Engineer, a B.Tech degree from IIT.

He invited Ajit and Sudha for his convocation function. Sudha requested Ajit to come alongwith her to Kharagpur. It was a pleasant surprise for Ajit, a bit hesitant but agreed to travel with her. The journey was good as it has to be as Sudha was with him on 24 hour basis. It was like a behavior of two opposite sex in a live in relationship.

During the convocation ceremony, Ishan was informed that he was also selected by an U.S. University for M.S., higher studies on a scholarship basis. He was supposed to do his Masters in Heat Transfer technology. He returned with them for a months and left for U.S. for his onward journey of education and professional career.

Sudha was quite upset as she never thought of leaving her son alone for U.S. But Ajit was a force behind to explain to her. Ajit told her that she has to behave like a responsible parent as his journey with her ends here and now onwards Ishan would have his life, his family. With a very heavy heart and faith in Ajit, she consoled herself.

Meanwhile, Prachee also completed her graduation and appeared to clear the IAS examination. She did not clear the examination in first attempt but never lost the hope and grit to appear for the second time. She asked Ajit, Uncle, since Ishan has left for U.S. and Mom is alone at home, would it be Ok, if I ask her to get me admitted in Rao's academy for one year for IAS Coaching? It was a difficult question for Ajit to answer but seeing her sincerity and also keeping the objective in view, he agreed to talk to Sudha but told Prachee, "the bottom line is this that you should pursue your passion and stand on a solid academic foundation."

Impossible is an expected word from Sudha but she only said, Ajit what would you have done in case, there was role reversal between you and me? Ajit said, he would have agreed to send her to Delhi and Kota because the goal and aim are both clear and defined in her mind. OK then you decide and advise her as she would be too happy to hear it from you. Of course I will remain present with you when you communicate to her.

She was sent to Delhi and Kota for one year. Ajit arranged everything right from paying guest accommodation to books etc. He also gifted her a scooty to travel from home to classes. Prachee was happy, Ajit was happy and so was Sudha.

Ajit could see a great sense of satisfaction in Sudha's eyes. Even he felt satisfied of doing part of his duties. Sudha was very close to saying that all this is done by a father. Are you listening Ajit? She hugged him and Ajit kissed her.

Ajit's helpless attraction to Sudha and later's desire to be able to live life on her terms took them to a tumultuous journey. This showed many layers of human nature including jealously, greed and pride. The entire journey was full of ideas of undying love, trust and loyalty, weaving an extra marital affairs and his heart became over imaginative and stupid. For a single mother, it is not only a daily financial but little domestic tasks which drain her both physically and mentally. She didn't get enough time with her children and this has caused some problems. Her being away for long hours did have an effect on kids. She was aware of that father's presence in house is important factor for healthy development of kids. While the son looks up to a father as a role model, the daughter's future relationship with the opposite sex is largely shaped by her interactions with her father and the image she has for him. Ajit has done this act to my satisfaction and I will remain ever grateful to him, said Sudha. Ajit did not actually understand clearly that Sudha was looking for a father to her kids. No doubt Ajit atleast behaved like one. The best part of Ajit in my life was that even my kids used to share their secrets with him rather than me. They trusted him more than I did. Then where is the gap between him and him? In fact he was taking and sharing all the responsibilities of a man of the family. He used to take good care of me. He made me emotionally strong. He is a real dude at 70 years and a hunk too. He said it once that he met a Hunk, Hunk said, I am a Hunk, so what said Ajit, I am a JAT. Yes he is darling too.

CHAPTER 22

ONE YEAR LATER

A healthy father daughter relationship is a mutually respectful open and honest communicative and trusting relationship where the daughter is confident in her father's enduring love, acceptance and belief in her ability to choose despite any mistake. Prachee was not Ajit's biological daughter but it was non too less than any ideal father daughter relationship.

She appeared in the IAS Entrance Examination and made Ajit proud of her hard work and determination. She was placed 90th in all India ranking. She passed the examination with flying colours. A month later she was sent for a regular training at Hyderabad.

She is more serious type so nothing much was explained to her as she had experienced in Delhi so Hyderabad was comparatively a nice and safe city to be trained.

After the training she got her first posting as Collector in MORENA district in Madhya Pradesh. Ajit and Sudha were a bit scared as the name sounded scary. One or two calls per day was a normal routine of both Ajit and Sudha. There were already lot of criminal activities happening there including the murders of senior police officers and burning cases of past Collectors by sand and stone mafia groups. Even the local politicians were mostly from outlaw class or with criminal background.

Ajit once told Prachee to come out of this area even if she had to resign. Her safety was the prime concern for Ajit and Sudha. Though Sudha never expressed it but he could see those lines of worry on her face.

Prachee was composed as if she was neither scared of nor bothered about the situation. She used to say that I will judge and act with no personal motive and always follow the path of truth which was more worrying for Sudha and Ajit. She stayed at MORENA for one year and was transferred to Bhopal as Secretary Urban Development as Secretary in Urban Department was good and she had opportunities to learn and prove. She was awarded the President's Medal for exemplary service and the city was beautified as never before.

Chapter 23

THIS IS CALLED COINCIDENCE.......

After one and half year in the month of January Prachee called up Ajit and said Ajit Uncle, I have something important to discuss with you which I am shit scared of discussing with Mom. Why are you not scared of discussing with me asked Ajit. Simple you will understand it impartially whereas Mom will think that I am a kid even after becoming IAS. Is it related to your marriage or what Ajit asked. How did you know, quipped Prachee. I can guess many things about you since I know you for so many years. I am not your biological father but you are a daughter to me since beginning. This is all the reason I am talking to you as I know that you are very important and responsible person in our lives including Mom.

Come to point I do not commit as your Mom thinks that I am spoiling you and Ishan but nevertheless, if I am convinced, I will try to convince Sudha. Let me know the entire details of your thoughts and actions. She started narrating the sequence of events. There is a guy called Avinash Mehra who was my batchmate at Hyderabad Academy, nice good looking boy with cultured manners and a decent respectable family. He is presently posted in

New Delhi as under Secretary to Home Ministry for System Improvement. His parents are based at Chandigarh and are from defence background, father retired as Brigadier. We have been knowing each other and have compatibility of nature and life. We have discussed and concluded that we can become husband and wife. In fact he has discussed with his parents and they have no problem in the acceptance.

CHAPTER 24

When Ishan informed that Ajit that he has an American girl friend and he could ask Mom to agree for a marriage in India as he does not believe in live in relationship. Ishan tried to convince Ajit on the basis of compatibility and explained the importance of mutual compatibility and understanding in marriage which he gauged to the extent possible before taking a final decision. Ajit Uncle please understand that this goes beyond castes, family background etc. I have spent close to one year with Anie and know her and we both have become emotional needs to each other. She has even told me to convert into HINDUISM if need be, but I have only told her to maintain her identity and just remain a good human being rather than Hindu, Christian or anybody.

Ajit told Sudha about this new development. He said Sudha, Ishan is a responsible boy. He is letting us know and seeking our blessings. He could have simply informed us after marriage then what you would have done? Respect his feelings. I am convinced that he has taken this step after a mutual thought.

Yes, they both find me easy to communicate so they do it. You also become like me with no ego, no fear, impartial. They would confide in you and I would love to see that change in you. In any case you also confide in me and not in your kids, so it would be better to accept their relationship and start preparations for the marriages of both Prachee and Ishan together and let me have that privilege of doing 'Kanyadan' of my so called adopted daughter. Now it is your turn to speak to Ishan and tell him to bring your daughter-in-law to be at home. Please always remember that the strongest people make time to help others even if they are struggling with their problems. Whereas they are our kids, Prachee is God's blessing to you and she would not only brighten our hearts but our whole world.

I know you have only spoilt them said Sudha to Ajit but with a body and eye movement of Sudha, Ajit could understand that she was loving every moment of their conversation and as usual Sudha hugged him and he kissed her. Their this relationship was undefined as usual and said that just remember that she can't put her arms around a memory so she just hugged someone, she loved today.

CHAPTER 25

MARRIAGES IN HOME

Gone are the days when white horses, carried the groom while Baraatis would dance throwing currency notes on him. Themed Baraat is new attraction in Indian Wedding. Punjabis are the people with a large heart, a love splendor and grandeur like any of the Indian marriage, Punjabi marriages are full of rituals and also full of fun and frolic. Keeping in mind the Punjabi culture and a high profile groom from Chandigarh, Ajit finalized some wedding planners from Mumbai. The planners were specifically advised to plan both the marriage celebrations together in Indian style. Anie is also to be treated as Ajit's daughter. Anie came to India alongwith Ishan last night only.

First ritual was ROKA Ceremony which was conducted for a commitment from both the aides, in this case from all the four sides which involved basically exchange of sweets, dry fruits and gifts.

Anie was dressed in a red saree for the first time and it was done by none other than her sister-in-law to be Prachee. She was looking stunning, beautiful and everyone present in the function, appreciated Ishan for a choice of a bride. She was behaving purely Indian and no American tantrums. Prachee as usual in a similar saree was also looking amazingly beautiful, these both girls presented a lovely scene of a Bollywood movie. Both the boys in their traditional Jodhpur suits were looking as if they have become ready for the marriage and not for ROKA only.

Everybody danced to the Bollywood songs except Ajit as first of all he was like Dharmendra of Indian movies, secondly he was genuinely busy overlooking all the arrangements. Next ritual was SAGAN which was arranged in the banquet hall of TAJ Inter-continental at New Delhi. This normally is done by the father of bride by applying Tilak on groom's forehead and offering gifts and sweets. Ajit did this job for both Prachee and Anie. Prachee's in-laws were very happy on Ajit's this gesture. This was followed by a ritual called 'Chunri Chadana' wherein groom's family visited bride house. The groom's sister presented a saree and the mother-in-law put a red Chunri on Prachee's head and gave her jewelry etc. Sudha did exactly same to ANNE.

UPTAN, the Haldi Ceremony was done to all Prachee, Ishan and ANNE in Sudha's house. Haldi was mixed with rose water and sandalwood to make a good paste. This was the first cosmetic make up for them. The skin of all three became soft and aromatic. For ANNE it was a wonderful experience as she never saw this type of fun in US. Lot of fun was created over there by married man and woman. Everybody joined into the fun of smearing their loved ones and got messy.

Sangeet ceremony was celebrated in the evening and continued till 1:00am. In fact it continued for many nights. Traditionally all the women married or single in the family gathered to dance and sing love songs and marriage songs. Though it was considered primarily a female show but males from both the families gatecrashed and danced to the fullest.

Two horses were decorated for Ishan and Avinash for baraat ceremony and both the parties had lot of guests and all danced in procession. Both the grooms were looking very handsome with their groom attire and Seharas, both the girls Prachee and ANNE after bridal make up were looking stunningly beautiful. Ajit managed the professional bride make-up artist from Oberoi Mumbai.

It was a scene to watch when garlands were exchanged between Prachee and Avinash, Ishan and ANNE. A big screen was arranged for a larger view of all the guests. The entire Shaadi rituals were done in Hindu vedic way. The lawns were brightly lit and a huge and elaborate dinner was arranged by Sudha. The menu selection was typically Punjabi and Continental for some high class society people. Sudha also invited all who is who of her industry.

The marriage got over by 4:00am. Ajit did 'Kanyadan' for both Prachee & ANNE. Now was the most difficult function. The Bidai of Prachee. The atmosphere suddenly became dull and everybody in Sudha's side started crying and weeping. By the time Sudha realized and started weeping like a kid, Prachee was sent to Airport with her husband and In-laws.

Before Sudha could further feel the absence of Prachee, Ajit reminded her that she had to Welcome ANNE & Ishan as even they have to leave for a week to Goa for honeymoon which was already arranged by Ajit.

The function got over. Both Ishan & ANNE had left for US and Prachee settled down nicely at Chandigarh with her in-laws.

Sudha now started feeling the heat of her loneliness and Ajit had to practically be on her side for few days.

Ajit told Sudha one day that Sudha it was nice to have done everything for the kids as a duty and now you can live by and for yourself. In the marriage functions, there were many suspicious eyes staring at me with a question why I had so much involvement? Why was I taking all the responsibility? and decisions? Why everyone right from the decorator to caterers, taking instructions from me? Because you are Ajit, the man who ....

CHAPTER 26

AFTER SIX MONTHS

For Sudha office business was as usual, so much of work and no time for her which made her more mechanical than an emotional lively female. Ajit was constantly searching the original Sudha in her and was always instigating her to take out a woman out of her rather than a business tycoon.

Ajit used to tell her about those little things, sunsets, coffee, long drives, their intercity business trips, giggles, sappy movies, ice creams, deep conversations and music. He used to say that these things are so little, yet mean a great deal to him. Even now they spark fire in our souls which no substance on earth can extinguish leaving you to burn with a passion for life. I have reached an age where my train of thoughts often leaves the station without me. Never forget who was there with you when no one else was. If you really love someone, even if there was a million reasons to leave, he would still look for the one reason to stay.

Why are you becoming a philosopher today and come to the point straight away Sudha asked? I could see and count few strands of grey hair across your ears so I was a bit worried, said Ajit. So how long would I be having those black thick hair? After all age rides over everyone sometimes, Sudha replied. But other aspects of your beauty including your assets have not changed and also the desire of mating, he asked with a mischievous smile on his face. Ajit, Are you asking me or telling me? I understand the impious hint of yours. Do you get me now?

Now listen to me very carefully, If you want something to last forever, you treat it differently. You shield it and protect it. You never abuse it. You don't expose it to the elements. You don't make it common or ordinary. If it ever becomes tarnished you lovingly polish it until it gleams like new. It becomes special, because you have made it so and it grows more beautiful and precious as time goes by.

Yes, I wil, I will, I always will, Ajit told Sudha. Ajit knew Sudha so well that he always used to say about her that women are strong not because they never break but because they know how to pick up pieces and put themselves together again.

Chapter 27

Sudha once told Ajit that now since the kids are settled. Ishan is in US and would not return for good. Prachee is in Chandigarh and she has her family and responsibility so more or less I am alone, why don't you come and stay with me? In live-in relationship or what Ajit asked? You can call it any name but purpose is that now we can stay together. Ajit said that few years back, when I suggested same thing to you, you said, Ajit you have only one aim whereas I have many. From that day I decided that I am with you all the time but I cannot afford to stay under the same roof as my self-respecting and unconditional love will become corrupt so I would rather stay away to maintain the sanctity of our relationship. I promised to myself to keep a safe physical distance between you and me but I do not know how would be the shape of things in the times to come.

Ajit, you have been integral part of my life and stood with me in thick and thin and even my kids have accepted you as a father figure in the family. Why can't we take it to the next level? Both the kids were telling me that they feel a little out of place to call you Ajit Uncle as you are with us in all our concerns. Why shouldn't we call him as Bade Paa. Sudha then got a shock of her life and thought to herself whether the kids have really understood the deep chemistry and our physical relationship, whether they have seen us in compromising position? She said think twice and you both decide yourselves. You both are sounding a bit out of place. I have no problem with this but once you do that it has to be respected in words and spirit. Yeah we agree Mom said both the kids in chorus. We also understand the seriousness of the relationship with him but you please ask Ajit Uncle whether he would agree to that and how would he react. I will also check with him, Sudha told.

Ajit, what is your take on this? I love and like the kids as much as you do. It has never come to my mind that they are not my kids. I am only not their biological father so I would love to be called Bade Papa by them. In fact this has added a little more responsibility on my shoulders. As far your question of staying together is concerned, give me some time to think as I have to decide on this issue after considering ethics, my desires. Normally I should have said that yes, I will shift right away as staying with you is a pleasant dream as I will not only have an emotional satisfaction but a physical satisfaction also. Since I love you to the core, I would not like to spoil you and would love to preserve you as a beautiful soul of my life. But I am not sure as the temptation and greed of being with you is weighing more than what is right and what's wrong. Yes, there is one thing for sure that I will stay with you when I want you in hours of my need.

Chapter 28

AFTER ANOTHER SIX MONTHS

Some people or couples experience a honeymoon phase shortly after retirement. A happy wife or a woman means a happy life for older man and better health in old age. If a person has ability to perform sex, it is a wonderful thing but always there comes time when it just can't happen, it is not the end of road. We all think, it's just related with ageing, No – Ajit thinks that when a man hasn't got a woman and he is sleeping by himself and he doesn't come in actual contact with a woman's body, he loses sexual feeling to a certain extent.

Considering and realizing the above factor of nature, Ajit became a bit thoughtful and decided to shift to Sudha's place. He also knew that Sudha is comparatively younger and she needs a man to stand guard against all her needs including emotions and natures.

They both agreed in principle without saying that they have reached an age where it wasn't quite like as it would have been in our late 20's, 30's or even 40's but they have to take the best use of their available resources and they were happy

89

complementing each other. There were few moments of frustrations also but they could deal with it.

There were many opportunities for the couple to enjoy their lives and to grow closer like the experience of increased travel and leisure time may be richer of shared. Also the partner on other hand provides extra ordinary companionship and support when health and mobility decline and the partner needs assistance. Ajit on one Sunday evening called Sudha in their balcony and asked her to sit and understand what he would advise. He started by saying that Sudha, now your business is established and you have people to look after day to day activities of your company. I suggest that you start attending your business needs only twice a week and rest of the time you utilize for your own development and for your own enjoyment of life. You have been longing for years together.

In order to bring a little discipline in your life, I have decided that we will go to see all the sensible dramas in any of the theatres in Delhi, we will not leave even one good restaurants without having meals there. We will go for unplanned long drives like Nainital, Shimla or elsewhere. We would go out for occasional movies. On weekends, we will have beer sitting in the same balcony.

I would also suggest you to develop your hobby for singing. If need be, you can also join some coaching classes. You have been very very irregular in going to your Beauty Parlours and Spa so let it be your regular feature. You are no doubt a beautiful female but it could still make you more beautiful. Remember I still have a very strong crush on you and that greed is still young and I am still not that old to perform. Are you listening to me Sudha? You will never improve, was the answer from Sudha. Do you remember I promised to myself that I will take out the real Sudha out of you when I joined your company years back? I am still determined to do so.

CHAPTER 29

AJIT SHIFTED TO SUDHA'S HOUSE

One fine morning he got a call from Sudha that she is suffering from high fever 103⁰F and having weakness and bodyache. It is suspected that she might be having dengu. Ajit without giving a second thought packed his baggage and shifted to Sudha's residence. He took her to the best hospital in South Bombay and admitted her inspite of Sudha's refusal. She wanted only a local treatment but sensing the seriousness of high temperature, he took the decision of not accepting what Sudha wanted.

Medical tests were conducted and it was confirmed that she had Dengu. Her blood plate count came down to 50,000 and still dropping. The hospital was not having the required blood to suit her group so Ajit ran from hospital to hospital from one blood bank to another blood bank and finally got the required blood from Bandra and she was given the required blood and medication.

Ajit stayed with her day and night and slept only for few hours. She was discharged after three days and brought home by Ajit. He even cooked food for her and himself even though he was having no knowledge of cooking. Only God

92

knew, what he ate, what he offered to Sudha 'but somehow' survived for two days before Sudha took the responsibility of kitchen and house.

After two more days he asked Sudha, whether he could move back to his house but Sudha caught hold of his hands and said, I am still not fully recovered and if you leave now, I will never recover nor I would like to recover. You have no choice but to stay and take care of me once forever. I am your baby and let baby not cry. Do you understand this Ajit? Yes baby, he stayed there on permanent basis for the rest of his life.

By now even the Society members also were not hostile and they started accepting Ajit as part of Sudha's life and a respectable member of that co-operative society where Sudha used to live. He even started getting invitations for birthday parties and society functions.

Next day evening Ajit took Sudha to Prithvi Theatre for a drama called Unfaithfully yours and spent a good time in watching the show and then had good dinner in Holiday Inn, Juhu. They returned late in the evening and they felt for the first time that they are husband and wife without marriage and social approval. The feeling of being so, gave immense pleasure to both of them.

Sudha was looking healthy now and Ajit was more romantic. Sudha asked him, why he liked her so much? What is so great about her? Ajit said, I see a thousand roses in this face, a million stars twinkling in these eyes and all the sunshine in this smile that can lit up the world and love the beauty of your being. You are just made for me, Sudha said and Ajit could feel that every time, he looks straight at her, she is a molten mess of nerves.

Yes, they were romantically so involved, that night that they didn't sleep till morning when the maid rang the doorbell to tell them that it is 8:00am. Sudha got ready and wore a pink Salwar Kurta and with a light make up, like eye liner and light shade of lipstick, she was looking stunningly gorgeous. It never appeared on her face that she did not sleep the whole night and body language also proved that she is not tired. Though Ajit was not involved in her company and business but he also joined her in the office after four hours sleep and it was like he had gone to her office just to bring her back home. They both returned home together and had a very refreshing hot tea together. Sudha wanted to relax for some time to compensate for the lack of sleep last night and told Ajit that there is a bed down there in the second bedroom and you can sleep there. Ajit very smartly answered that he is in habit of sleeping only in the master bed room. You only have a devils eye on me and know how to get your way in, said Sudha to Ajit. Ok, whatever and they both slept on the same bed. Soon they found themselves on the bed three feet of distance between them and sharing the same quilt. Ajit was acting for being slept and trying to touch her. Sudha gave him the quilt and took another blanket. Even then the knowledge of her bare feet sent sense of mischief in his mind and his heart started beating harder. Sudha tried her best to dissuade Ajit to let her be at her own but this guy was almost out of his own controls. He said, Sudha even without make up and faint lipstick you are looking beautiful. Sudha is a human being so she surrendered to his charm. Her skin became real and soft. They had to get up only at 10:00pm for the purpose of cooking. While cooking, she asked Ajit where do you get this much of energy at this age? Is it because, you have eaten so much o Ghee or what? No – I am like, Baali of Ramayan, I naturally get half the 'Shakti' (energy) from you so mathematically. I am stronger than you with a margin of my individual energy as your energy is equally divided between you and me so this is the reason, do you understand Sudha? Yeah, you have answer for everything on earth but you are a cute darling too.

Ajit told Sudha that I may not be the most important person in your life but I just hope that one day when you hear, remember my name, you would just smile and say, I miss you. Yes, I will miss you Sudha said and also told Ajit that I have come to realize that the only people I need in my life are the ones who need me in their's even when I have nothing else to offer, you are the one.

Sudha was in kitchen doing some cooking and Ajit followed her there and wanted to share some of Sudha's domestic work and he realized that participation in domestic work leads to intimacy and more sex in relationship. Though Sudha never had a grouse that Ajit should help in kitchen work, but Ajit felt that if he didn't do this, this would leave her feeling, angry and tired as she already had a hectic work schedule ad he thought that he needs to break his old school thought. This left a feeling of being supported, cared for and loved and Ajit was a winner, as he got Sudha in toto. Sudha actually forgot that she ever was a poor widow.

Ajit had to travel to Calcutta for a week for some family function. It was difficult for Sudha to see him away for such a long time according to her. While both being away both started sexting a social and technological phenomenon changing the dynamics of their relationship. Ajit thought that rather than wasting a lot of mental and emotional energy worrying about whether Sudha likes or approves of him he took a moment to analyze if what he was feeling inside all the butterflies, adrenalin and excitement was simply chemical. If you got lost in feeling of lust you could easily end up in a toxic relationship. Ajit knew his limits of the relationship so he was a happy person and he made Sudha also happy by understanding her needs and psychological requirements. He was happy with Sudha because he chose a person with a positive attitude and not a rigid wood. Sudha also knew that her body is built with a sixth sense to other people's energies and intentions and she paid close attention to all warning signals her not to fall to a toxic or dramatic relationship. She also knew that if she felt drained after Ajit leaves, this will be a signal that this relationship with Ajit is mutually beneficial. Benefit being that they both are complimentary to each other. The company at this junction is purely a compatibility mathematics. Ajit returned and Sudha celebrated.

In the evening they both went to Prithvi Theatre to see a play written, directed and enacted by Anupam Kher. The play was simply outstanding. The play was of a autographical satire. Sitting at the back, realizing how far away from the stage they were and yet were mesmerized by the entire experience and power of the theatre to reach the audience.

Overall they enjoyed the show and hot Samosas of Prithi canteen. Late evening, they reached home and had dinner together which was cooked by Sudha before going for a drama.

During conversation Sudha casually asked Ajit whether he had visited Bangkok, Pattaya, Phuket and if yes what all he did there? Ajit knowing fully well what Sudha wanted to hear, said that there is no point explaining you where did I go and what all I did in Bangkok, I will take you to all these places and explain to you in person for better understanding. I know what are you trying to convey Ajit but you won't succeed in your intended pursuits. Ok, let us see but yes, you gave me an idea and I have decided to take you on an old age Honeymoon to Bangkok in next 4 weeks, I will see, said Sudha.

CHAPTER 30

AFTER ONE YEAR

Finding Ajit dull, Sudha asked him how are you feeling today. I can see some old smile on your face. Why can't you share it Ajit?

Ajit - I am feeling better, I can see the clear blue sky and can also see you pretending to be happy. I do not really know with which material God has created you. You are strong beautiful same as you were 20 years ago when I met you and actually saw you. Do you remember that we were out on an official trip to Chandigarh? Sudha nods and smiles but Ajit could see the depth of anticipated tragedy in her eyes.

Ajit calls her up but there was no response, may be she is busy in kitchen, Ajit gets irritated and shouts again for her. She comes and says what happened Baba?

Sudha listen I have been busy throughout my life in meetings. Today you please arrange two meetings for me. One with my staff and other with my elder daughter. Younger one will not like to meet me as he is of firm belief that his Papa was at fault for all the mess in the family. He should have joined us in US. Yes, the elder one still believes that Papa can't be wrong. There will definitely be some reasons for him to do so and stay back in DELHI. I am sure that my wife will never ever agree to see me as she had to stay alone with the kids in US and Ajit could not reach her even when she was seriously ill.

Sudha agreed to arrange both the meetings and assured Ajit that she would do her best if at all it could be made possible. The first meeting was easy so it was done within a week. Ajit addressed the first meeting.

FIRST MEETING –

Guys, Thank you very much for all the support and trust in me, in my company and in your Managing Director, Sudha madam. Today I am finally retiring and will not be available for any advice from me or from you to me. Please continue the same efforts and ensure that this MD doesn't miss me even for a moment. This is going to be your best send off to me. God bless.

SECOND MEETING –

It was arranged after two weeks. It all started like – Nidhi, I have always tried to be a good father and also been successful. Since you are the eldest in the family I would express my last desire and request you to take care of your MAA and little brother. As far as responsibility of a father and husband is concerned, I have tried to do them the best possible. I may have faulted in some duties but again I am a human being. I am sure you will carry my legacy to the way I dreamt of. I could also see your younger brother in one corner of this room probably thinking that his Papa was right in a way and he was not all that wrong. One more thing, Nidhi, you let your MAA know that even though I am staying in Sudha's place but your Mom remains my life even now and relationship between me and Sudha has always been with a mutual respect and never like husband and wife.

NOW TO SUDHA –

You have always been part of my life, a support system, a balanced soul to advise me from and stopping me for committing physical and emotional blunders. My love to you for all these years has been absolutely without any selfish motive with an idea of give not take. I have enjoyed every moment of this period. Before the memory becomes weak eyes fragile, strength Zero, limited breath, I confirm that I love you to the core of my heart and with the purity of soul. If we all believe in rebirth, I would like to be reborn as your soul mate.

I HAVE A LAST WISH –

Please change my Bed sheet, Pillow Covers to absolute white. I am tired. I want to rest in peace. My eyes are becoming heavy. I am now seeing illusions.

But before I go in deep slumber, if God can provide me a moment to see you saying that he was not a cheater and his presence had become a habit of my life and God has cheated me for the second time.

Tears rolled down and that man Ajit became a body. TIME doesn't wait for anybody, anything.

Printed in the United States
By Bookmasters